The Most Important Christmas

by James H. Nelesen
illustrated by Carolyn Ewing Bowser

CPH.
SAINT LOUIS

Every spelling word Mrs. Torres gave the class made Emily think of Christmas.

"Letter," Mrs. Torres said and Emily thought of the stack of brightly colored Christmas cards on the table at home.

"Perfect," said Mrs. Torres and Emily thought of how perfectly charming she would look when she played the part of Mary in the Christmas program at church.

"Color," her teacher said and Emily thought of blue, the blue dress she would wear as her costume.

"Never," Mrs. Torres said and Emily thought of two long weeks of school until the big night.

Copyright ©1985 Concordia Publishing House
3558 S. Jefferson Avenue, St. Louis, MO 63118-3968
Manufactured in the United States of America

Library of Congress Cataloging in Publication Data

Nelesen, James H., 1937-
    The most important Christmas.

    Summary: After not being chosen for the important role of Mary in the school Christmas program, Emily learns about the true spirit of the holiday.
    1. Children's stories, American. [1. Christmas—Fiction.   2. Christian life—Fiction]   I. Title.
PZ7.N4296Mo 1985   [E]   84-23037
ISBN 0-570-04110-4

    5   6   7   8   9   10   11   12   03   02   01   00   99   98   97

Emily was sure Mrs. Torres would choose her to play the part of Jesus' mother because Emily had practiced for it. She had studied all the pictures of Mary on all the Christmas cards that had come in the mail at home. So Emily knew how Mary's hands were supposed to be folded when she looked down at Jesus asleep on the hay. She also knew how Mary was supposed to kneel when the shepherds came to the stable. Emily also knew how Mary was supposed to smile when the Wise Men gave her gifts for her baby.

Emily was the only girl in the class with a baby brother, so she was the only one who knew how to hold a baby the way a real mother would.

And, of course, Emily had a blue dress to wear as a costume, the same color as the dress Mary wore in all the Christmas pictures.

Mrs. Torres would *have* to choose Emily, and this was the day she would announce it to the class.

And that was why Emily started to cry before recess.

"It was very hard to decide," Mrs. Torres said, "but I would like to ask Jennifer Mosconi to play the part of Mary in the Christmas program and Hector Oliva to be Joseph."

For one second Emily thought something had gone wrong with her ears because, when Mrs. Torres had said "Emily Morgan," it had sounded like "Jennifer Mosconi."

For another second Emily thought Mrs. Torres had made a mistake and had read the wrong name.

But the next second Emily knew that it was true. She had not been chosen to play the most important part in the Christmas program.

Mrs. Torres announced the names of the boys who would be shepherds and Wise Men and told the rest of the class that they would be the angel chorus.

Emily really didn't hear Mrs. Torres explain how important angels were in the Christmas story by telling about the one who announced to Mary that she would be the mother of the Savior of the world. Nor did Emily care about the wondrous choir of angels who appeared to the shepherds as they kept watch over their flocks by night and who sang "Glory to God in the highest" and said "Go to Bethlehem where you will see the Baby wrapped in swaddling cloths, lying in a manger."

Instead, Emily pretended to be looking for something way in the back of her desk so no one could see her crying.

From that moment on, everything seemed to go wrong for Emily.

During recess the boys threw snowballs at the girls the way they always did. Even though Emily told them she wasn't playing, she got snow down her boot when they chased her anyhow.

During art period Mrs. Torres showed the class how to make snowflakes by cutting folded pieces of paper, but Emily's came out almost round and wavy instead of pointed and fancy like everyone else's.

And just before the bell rang at the end of the day, the class drew names for their Christmas gifts. Emily drew Charles Hoffman's name. Charles' parents were rich, so he had every toy there was in the world. Now Emily had to buy him a present for less than two dollars.

"Be sure to tell your parents the part you'll play in the Christmas program," Mrs. Torres said. "That will give them time to help you make your costume."

Emily didn't care about her costume. She was going to be stuck in the angel chorus and would wear a plain white sheet instead of her blue dress.

When Emily got home she didn't ask her mother if any more Christmas cards had come in the mail.

She didn't run into the kitchen and ask her mother if she could hold her baby brother, Daniel.

Instead, she walked slowly into the kitchen where her mother was cooking dinner and where Daniel was playing in his play pen.

Mrs. Morgan saw that Emily was sad. "What's the matter?" she asked.

"Nothing," Emily answered.

"Then would you hold Daniel a while?" she said.

"I guess so," Emily said.

Daniel played with his rattle as he sat in Emily's lap and Mrs. Morgan stirred a pot on the stove. It was very quiet in the kitchen.

"Mrs. Torres asked Jennifer to be Mary in the Christmas program," Emily said suddenly.

"I'm sure Jennifer will be very good in that part," Emily's mother said.

"But she doesn't know how Mary's supposed to fold her hands or kneel. And she doesn't know how to hold a baby like a real mother. And she probably doesn't even have a blue dress," Emily said.

"Well, she will have lots of time to practice," Mrs. Morgan answered. "The program is still two weeks away."

Emily's mother took some dishes from the cabinet and began setting the table.

"It's the most important part in the Christmas program," Emily said softly. "I wanted to be Mary," she said, even more softly.

Emily's mother had finished setting the table and put Daniel in his high chair.

"You know what's so wonderful about Christmas?" she said. "It's the one time of the year when people think about others instead of themselves."

Mrs. Morgan began feeding Daniel his baby food.

"We give each other gifts," she continued, "instead of buying things for ourselves."

Emily gave Daniel a spoonful of baby food as her mother got up to stir something that was cooking on the stove.

"I think the people in the Christmas story started it," Emily's mother continued. "Mary and Joseph didn't mind sleeping in a stable as long as their baby was safe and warm. The shepherds didn't mind walking into town late at night because they were thinking about the Savior that had been born there. And the Wise Men didn't think about how tired they would be after traveling so far. They were thinking of the child who was really a king."

Mrs. Morgan finished feeding Daniel.

"But the most important person in the Christmas story is Jesus," she said. "And He didn't mind being born as an ordinary baby even though He was really the Son of God. That was because He was thinking about us instead of Himself."

Emily thought about what her mother had said as she brought a wet cloth to wipe Daniel's hands.

She thought about it on Saturday, too, when her father took her shopping for a gift for Charles that wouldn't cost more than two dollars.

And she was still thinking about it as she got ready for school on Monday.

Sale 1⁹⁹

SUPER
SAUCERS

"I have to have an angel costume," she said as she got into the car, carrying her books, her lunch box, and a large paper bag. "But I don't need to bring it to school until next week."

"I suppose we can find something to make you look like an angel," Mother said as she buckled Daniel into his car seat. "By the way, what's in the bag?" she asked.

"A costume, but it's not for me," Emily answered. "It's my blue dress. I'm going to ask Jennifer if she wants to wear it."

"I'm sure she will," Emily's mother said and she smiled as she started the car to take Emily to school.

The End